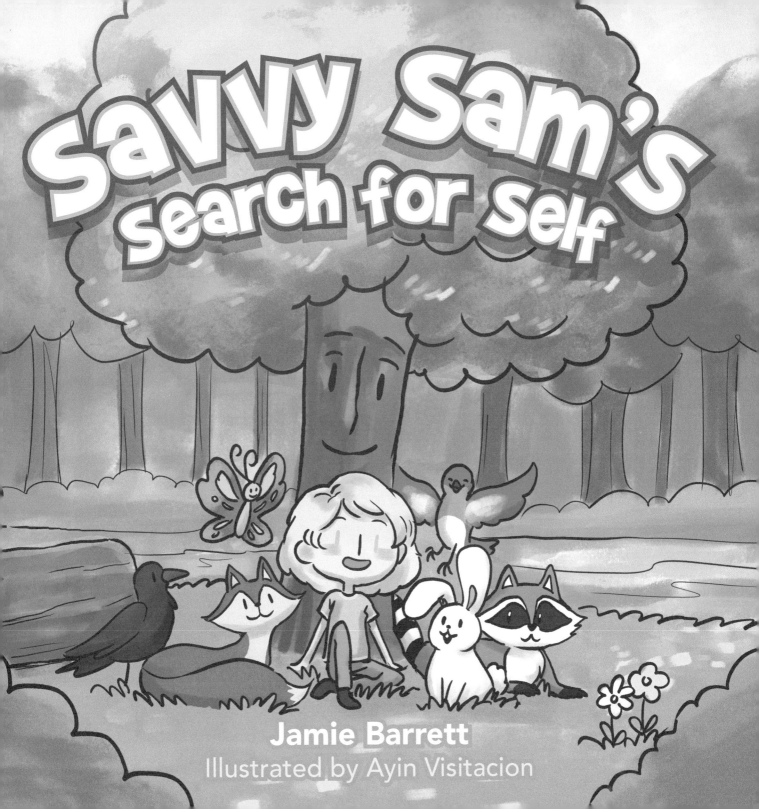

Savvy Sam's Search for Self

Jamie Barrett

Illustrated by Ayin Visitacion

Balboa Press books may be ordered through booksellers or by contacting:

Balboa Press
A Division of Hay House
1663 Liberty Drive
Bloomington, IN 47403
www.balboapress.com
1 (877) 407-4847

ISBN: 978-1-9822-4055-4 (sc)
978-1-9822-4054-7 (e)

Print information available on the last page.

Balboa Press rev. date: 12/27/2019

BALBOA.PRESS
A DIVISION OF HAY HOUSE

This book is dedicated to my amazing daughter, Lindsey.

Savvy Sam went to sit under a special tree,

It gave awe-inspiring advice.

Yes sir ree, Yes sir ree.

Oh, Sassafras Tree, so wise and so free.

Please tell me, oh please,

How to be more me.

Who am I?

What is my identity?

Sassafras Tree whispers out on a breeze,

You are not your mind my friend.

Your thoughts aren't even real, you see.

You are the observer of all that you think,

And all that you feel.

You can change your thoughts if need be,

Especially if you think negatively.

Oh really, oh really, oh really wise tree?

Envelop me in your philosophy.

So, if I think I cannot do something,

I tell myself to STOP this thinking?

What are you thinking right now Savvy Sam?

Tell me the thoughts you have right now, so profound.

I am thinking I can't,

Draw like Drew,

Or run like Rita,

Or paint like Paul,

Or read like Reeva.

I am thinking oh wise tree so green, brown, and buff,

That I'm just NOT GOOD ENOUGH!

9

Savvy Sam, Listen well… Change that belief,

And get rid of that spell.

Pelt, peel, and pull that belief right out.

Get rid of rude Rosey, the dead dreaded doubt.

Most all people have that fear,

Wake up to NOW and choose to cheer.

It's a disease you see and exists in all,

Whether thin, big, small, tall or all at the mall.

Say this NOW. Say it after me.

I AM GOOD ENOUGH. I love me.

I deserve to be happy for eternity.

I've always been good enough.

I'm good enough right now.

I choose to believe this.

And make it my vow.

Be present right now.

Give yourself this gift.

Live life, make a change.

Past and future are out of range.

Leave behind all the mind chatter.

Pitter patter, pitter patter,

It really does matter.

Like rain wash away negative thinking.

As it rises up, make it go in a blinking.

And if someone says something that's really mean;

Best to just go eat a bowl of butter beans.

Feel sad or mad; Don't deny what you feel;

Take responsibility to help yourself heal.

Release the hurt, the sad, mad, or fear.

Help your mind and body be clear.

Learn the lesson from what happened,

And don't continue to feel saddened.

Release bad thoughts that don't serve you well.

Replace them with good ones,

And you will feel so swell.

And lastly be crafty about who you are,

Raise the bar.

Remember a time you felt sudden awe, wonder and bliss.

Take time to remember and reminisce.

You are that feeling that you recall.

From one of those times at a wondrous waterfall.

That's who you are, that feeling you feel.

The wonder and awe and,

Blessed bliss so real.

Mind stay quite so I can be,

Present and live right now,

And be me!

Thank you, so much wise Sassafras Tree.

I'm grateful to you for helping me,

Find my own identity.

I deeply and completely accept myself,

I love me.

Affirmations

The only power I have, are the choices I make right NOW, in the now, in the moment.

The Past and Future are out of range.

All I have is NOW.

I live more fully right now, in the now, in the moment.

I make positive choices for myself right now.

I'm aware of what my thoughts are.

My thoughts are not who I am.

I can change my thoughts if my thoughts are not good for me.

I never deny what I'm thinking. I can change negative thoughts into positive thoughts.

My feelings are not who I am.

Feelings come up in waves and just are.

All feelings are alright.

It's not bad to have negative feelings.

I accept the feelings I feel. I never deny a negative feeling.

I'm able to release a negative feeling by accepting
the feeling and talking about it.

I can release negative feelings in healthy ways.

I deeply and completely love and accept myself.

I choose to be self-confident.

I choose to be successful today.

I choose to be kind.

I choose to forgive.

I forgive myself to release guilty feelings.

I choose to forgive others to release anger or hurt feelings.

When I forgive others, it doesn't mean what they did is
okay. It means I can release my anger, hurt, or pain.

I choose to be happy.

I do whatever it takes to be happy right NOW.

I am responsible for my own happiness.

I am sensitive to how others feel.

I choose to be assertive. I tell people what I want or need from them.

I listen to my friends.

I am a good friend.

I describe what I see and hear, smell, or feel to ground
myself back to the present moment.

I live in a space of now in awe and wonder of creation all around me.

I am the true essence of the feeling of awe and wonder, bliss, and peace.

I have a positive attitude.

I choose the courage to tell the truth about my thoughts and my feelings.

I choose happiness right NOW.

References

The Institute for Rapid Resolution Therapy by Dr. Jon Connelly.

Emotional Freedom Technique, Energy Psychology Technique by Gary Craig.

Originally from Mississippi, Jamie Barrett is a psychotherapist who currently resides in Mount Dora, FL. She is in private practice, owns her own company, and provides contract services for Total Life Counseling, Inc. She utilizes hypnotherapy and energy psychology among some of her services.

During Jamie's internship, she enrolled in the Choctaw American Indian Pearl River Reservation program through their social services agency. She was later offered the position of a Handicap Coordinator working with Choctaw Indians of all ages with mental health issues and physical limitations.

Jamie has had Advanced Forensic Interview training from APSAC (American Professional Society on the Abuse of Children). She has extensive experience in interviewing children who are allegedly child abuse victims and has testified as an expert in the Criminal and DCF Dependency Courts, as well as the Family Court System. Jamie attended the Play Therapy Training Institute in Hackensack, NJ to pursue credits to obtain Certification as a Registered Play Therapist - Supervisor.

Jamie has extensive training and experience working with children and adult victims of sexual and physical abuse, parental neglect, and domestic violence. Jamie was the Team Coordinator for the Child Protection Team for Lake and Sumter Counties. Jamie contracted with the Lake County Head Start preschool program to conduct play therapy service for their children who were referred to play therapy through a company she created, Play 4 Goodness Sake, Inc. Jamie also provided classroom observation and Consultation services for the agency.

Jamie has been a Clinical Supervisor for a not for profit children's agency. She supervised counselors and Interns as well as Forensic Counselors. Jamie has supervised The Forensic Interviewing program and she developed the Play Therapy Program at the Children's Advocacy Center.

Ms. Barrett's hobbies are traveling, studying, spending time with her daughter and playing with Gizmo, her incorrigible long haired chihuahua.

Printed in the United States
By Bookmasters